S 031003

S 031003

Adams, Pam
Mrs. Honey's Dream

DATE DUE		
JUN 1 0 2008		
JUN 2 2 2009		
JUN 1 5 2010		
JUN 2 9 2010		
JUN 0 6 2011		
JUL 1 0 2015		
OCT 1 0 2017		
SEP 1 1 2018		
OCT 1 6 2018		
AUG 2 7 2019		

D1279780

It was a warm, sunny day.
Mrs Honey fell asleep
in her deckchair.

Thomas the cat was asleep
on her lap.

They were both dreaming . . .

Thomas dreamt
he was flying.

He was enjoying himself.
Suddenly, he saw a strange bird.

"It looks very big,"
he said to himself. "Help!"

He looked again and saw
that it wasn't a bird at all.
It was Mrs Honey
flying through a cloud.

Mrs Honey dreamt
she was flying.

She was surprised
to see Thomas flying below her
and waved to him
with her knitting.

Suddenly, Thomas started to fall . . .
Down, down, down into the ocean.

Splash!

Thomas dreamt
he was surrounded
by huge, fierce fish.

They had enormous, sharp teeth
and glaring eyes.

Thomas tried to scream,
but he couldn't find his voice.

"Help!" he squeaked.

Mrs Honey dreamt
she went to rescue Thomas.

"I'm coming, Thomas,"
she called.

She shook her knitting needles
angrily at the fish.
They swam off,
looking very cross.

Thomas dreamt
he was rescued by Mrs Honey.

"Thank you," he said.
"I like fish, but not
when they are that big!"

Thomas looked around.
"I can't swim," he cried.

"Neither can I for very long,"
said Mrs Honey. "I hope
someone rescues us soon."

Mrs Honey dreamt
she and Thomas
were caught in a big net.

Sailors pulled them
out of the water
and lifted them
on board their ship.

Thomas dreamt
he landed on the deck
of a sailing ship.

He sat in a puddle
of water.

"Here is a saucer of milk,"
said the captain.
"It was lucky for you
that we saw you!"

Mrs Honey dreamt
the captain offered her
a glass of lemonade.

"Thank you for saving us,"
she said. "Shall I bake you
some cakes?"

"Yes, please," said the captain.
"May I lick out the bowl?
Yum, yum!"

Thomas dreamt
he saw a pirate ship
sailing towards them.

"Ship, ahoy. . ." he called.
But the sailors were so busy
eating cakes, they didn't hear.

At last, the captain looked up.

"Help! It's Captain Bones
and his horrible rabble!"

Mrs Honey dreamt
the pirates were climbing
up the rigging.

They waved their cutlasses
in the air.

Mrs Honey fought them
with her knitting needles.

But they were too many.

Thomas dreamt
he ran up the rigging
to escape the pirates.
He was scared...

Luckily, the pirates
had seen the cakes.
Soon, there wasn't
a single one left.

"More cakes! More cakes!"
bellowed the pirates.

Mrs Honey dreamt
she told the pirates,
"Don't be greedy.
I've used all the eggs.
I can't make any more cakes."

"In that case, we will make you
and your cat walk the plank,"
sneered Captain Bones.

" Cats bring bad luck."

Thomas and Mrs Honey
woke up with a start.

It was raining. They were wet
and the deckchair had collapsed.

"I had a dream about pirates,
Thomas," said Mrs Honey.
"You were in it, too.
I wonder what happened
to those pirates."

"Miaow," said Thomas.
He knew.

Dream a story Competition

Take turns to dream
a story with your family,
friends or classmates.

The best entries will win a set of
Mrs Honey stories for your school.

Entries to Child's Play,
Ashworth Road, Swindon, England, SN5 7YD

Australian entries to Child's Play,
5/53 Myoora Road, Terrey Hills, NSW 2084